JANE AND THE PIRATES

Jules Older

Illustrated by
MICHAEL BRAGG

HEINEMANN:LONDON

William Heinemann Ltd
10 Upper Grosvenor Street, London W1X 9PA

LONDON · MELBOURNE · TORONTO
JOHANNESBURG · AUCKLAND

First published 1984

A school pack of BANANAS 1–6
is available from
Heinemann Educational Books
ISBN 0 435 00100 0

434 93020 2
Printed in Italy by
Imago Publishing Ltd

Chapter One

Once upon a time, long, long ago and far, far away, there lived a girl named Jane. Jane lived in a village by the sea.

One day, when Jane was on her way to school, she looked out across the harbour and there she saw, far off in the distance, a sailing ship. Now Jane was very interested in ships so she stopped for a while and, though she was already a little late for school, she watched the ship sail towards town. As it drew closer she saw that it was a three-masted sailing ship with white sails and a dark flag fluttering from the top of the main mast.

1

I wonder what that is, she thought,
and she climbed onto a barrel standing in
front of a shop for a better look. The ship
grew closer and closer. Suddenly Jane's

2

eyes opened wide; she saw that the dark
flag on top of the mast was the Jolly
Roger—the skull and crossbones! It's a
pirate ship, she thought, and it's coming
here to burn our village and steal the
people's money and gold.

From the top of the barrel, Jane turned
back towards the town and yelled with all
her might, 'Pirates! Pirates! Pirates are
coming! Pirates are coming!' Doors and
windows flew open. Townspeople stuck
their heads out and looked in horror as
the ship approached the dock.

*Will the pirates raid the village? Will the
people heed Jane's cry? Read Chapter
Two—and find out!*

Chapter Two

JANE'S CRY WAS taken up from street to street. 'Turn out! The pirates are coming!'

From out of every house ran women and men armed with guns and sabres, even pitchforks and brooms. Farmers rushed from their fields, sailors jumped off their boats, fishermen gathered up their catch and ran to shore in order to do battle with the pirates. The school teacher rushed from her blackboard, grabbed her pointer and ran towards the wharf.

They all got there just in time. The pirate ship sailed up to the wharf and quickly lowered its gangplank. The pirates gathered on deck. One of them jumped on the railing to lead the charge.

It was Captain Redbeard, the meanest
pirate who sailed the seas.

Redbeard and his men came tumbling
off the ship. They were mighty surprised
to see all the people ready for them.
Redbeard had told them that they would

be able to sneak quietly into town and steal all the money and gold. But the people were waiting and a terrible fight ensued. Slick-slack! Snick-snack! Kow! Pow! Pirates and townspeople fought and fought, some falling into the water, others being chased through the streets. Jane watched from the top of her barrel at the battle raging all around her.

Suddenly, Jane felt a horrible, hot hand reach around her neck. An evil voice growled, 'Now, little lady, you are my prisoner!'

Whose evil voice is this? Why is Jane being taken prisoner? Read Chapter Three – and find out!

Chapter Three

JANE GASPED AS she felt herself being lifted off the barrel. She twisted around and was horrified to find that the man with the evil voice was none other than

the awful leader of the pirates, Captain
Redbeard. He carried her under his arm
through the crowd and up the gangplank
of the ship. 'Follow me, mates!' he called
to his pirate crew.

Those who were left fought their way back onto the ship. 'It was this little girl,' snarled Redbeard, 'who warned the townspeople we was coming. I was watching her through me spyglass. Well, now she'll cook for us and clean for us and be our prisoner for the rest of her life.' And he laughed a horrible laugh.

'Help!' cried Jane. 'Help! Help! The pirates are taking me prisoner.'

She looked back as Redbeard held her tight in his grip. Jane saw her mother and father racing towards her through the crowd. Through the streets they ran and onto the wharf, desperately trying to save her. But just as they reached the ship, the pirates pulled up the gangplank and sailed out to sea.

The Captain threw Jane down on the deck and stood over her until the village was out of sight. Then he left her. Jane wept bitterly. How awful to be the prisoner of these cruel pirates! She thought of her mother and father, whom she might never see again.

Just then she heard a voice whisper behind her, 'Don't be afraid.'

Will Jane ever see her mother and father again? And who is whispering to her? Read Chapter Four—and find out!

Chapter Four

'WHO'S THAT?' GASPED Jane.

'I'm Tim. I'm the cabin boy,' answered the voice.

Jane turned around. Behind her knelt a boy not much older than she. 'Oh, you awful pirate,' she said. 'You tried to attack our town.'

'No, no! I'm not a pirate. I was captured just as you were when the pirates raided the town where I lived. They took me prisoner when their last cabin boy escaped. I've been a prisoner on this ship for nearly six months now. And I swear I'm not a pirate.'

'Then why didn't you yell out when you saw them coming to our town?' Jane asked. 'You could have warned us.'

'Because before the pirates raid a town

they lock me down in the brig.'

'The brig – what's a brig?'

'Oh, that's what they call a jail on a boat,' Tim explained. 'And "galley" is the word for kitchen. You'll learn all about life on board ship,' he added, slowly, 'because I'm afraid we're here for the rest of our lives.'

'Never!' said Jane. 'We must escape, Tim!'

Just then they heard the sound of

heavy boots. It was Captain Redbeard.
He bent down so that his face was right in
front of Jane's. He looked straight into
her eyes. 'And don't be thinking of
escaping,' he said as if he had read her
mind. 'You'll never escape from this
ship, little girl.' And he laughed a cruel
laugh. 'Ha ha ha ha ha.'

*Will Jane and Tim escape? Or will they
remain prisoners for ever? Read Chapter
Five – and find out!*

Chapter Five

WEEKS WENT BY. Jane and Tim were kept busy waiting on the pirates while they ate their meals and cleaning up after them when they had finished. The ship was far out to sea, and there was no chance at all for escape.

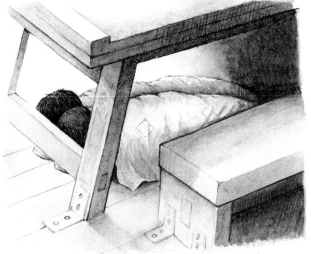

At night they had no bed but had to sleep in the galley, either on the table or, when the sea was rough, underneath it.

For covers they each had only one thin blanket. Life on board ship was cruel, but because they had each other to talk to and to hold on to on cold nights, they never gave up.

One morning after breakfast, Jane and Tim were cleaning the galley when they heard, from high atop the mast, the call, 'Ship ahoy!' Along with every man in the crew, they rushed on deck. The pirate on watch in the crow's nest had spotted a ship way out on the horizon. 'Perhaps it's a warship come to rescue us,' whispered Jane to Tim.

'I hope so,' said Tim. 'But I'm afraid it's not.'

As the ship drew closer, they discovered that Tim was right. It was a merchant ship carrying passengers and probably filled with gold and silver.

'What will happen now, Tim?'

'The pirates will trick them into thinking that we're another merchant ship. They'll come alongside us to exchange greetings, and then Redbeard will hoist the Jolly Roger and attack them. They won't stand a chance.'

'Tim, we must stop him. Redbeard will kill the passengers just to get their money.'

'But we can't,' Tim answered. 'There's no way.'

'If only we could warn them,' said Jane thoughtfully.

The ship grew closer and closer to the pirates. 'If we don't think of something soon,' whispered Tim, 'they are doomed!'

Will the merchant ship fall into Redbeard's trap? Can Jane and Tim find a way to save them? Read Chapter Six – and find out!

Chapter Six

THE MERCHANT SHIP steered right into Redbeard's trap. Little did they know they were approaching not another merchantman, but a pirate ship! Already the two vessels were so close that Jane could make out the smiling faces of the passengers as they waved to them from the deck. 'We must let them know that this is a pirate ship, Tim,' she said. 'Soon they'll be right alongside us, and then the pirates will launch the attack.'

'But how?' asked Tim. 'How can we do it?'

'I've got an idea!' exclaimed Jane. 'Quick, Tim, follow me!'

She led him along the deck to the main mast of the ship. At the foot of the mast lay the pirate flag, the Jolly Roger. It was hitched to a line waiting to be run up the mast as soon as the trap was sprung.

The pirates were all busy getting ready for the attack, and no one noticed as Jane grabbed the line that held the pirate flag. Quick as she could, she pulled the line, hand over hand, and quickly raised the flag up to the top of the mast. As soon as it was fluttering in the breeze, she and Tim raced down to the galley and made themselves appear very busy washing dishes.

They looked out of the galley porthole and watched the reactions of the people on the merchant ship to the Jolly Roger. They saw them point to the pirate flag and then watched as the ship sharply and suddenly changed its course. It steered away from the pirate ship, away to the horizon and to safety. Jane and Tim had saved the passengers and crew.

Above them, on the deck, they could hear Captain Redbeard stomping angrily about in his big boots. 'Which of you scurvy lot ran that flag up the mast? Which one was it then? Be quick and tell me!' he shouted. But no one answered. Then they heard Redbeard's boots clomp, clomp, clomp down the ladder to the galley where Jane and Tim shivered in fear.

Will Redbeard suspect his two prisoners? Will he discover that it was Jane who warned the merchant ship? And what will he do to her if he does? Read Chapter Seven—and find out!

Chapter Seven

TIM AND JANE heard Redbeard ask the cook whether he had run the flag up the mast and then heard the cook's frightened answer, 'No, sir, not I.'

Redbeard stalked into the galley where Jane and Tim were shakily trying to clean plates. He went right over to Tim. 'And was it you, me lad, what run up the Jolly Roger and warned the merchant ship?' he asked, with rage quivering in his voice.

So frightening was the Captain that Tim knew he could never lie to him. But he remembered that it was actually Jane who had the idea, and Jane who pulled the flag to the top of the mast. So, swallowing hard, he answered truthfully, 'No, sir, not I.'

Then Redbeard looked down at Jane as she sat with a tin plate in her hand. She too felt she would be unable to lie to the fierce pirate. But his face showed what he was thinking. Why, this is just a little girl. She couldn't think of a trick like that. And even if she thought of it, she could never do it. He sneered down at her for a moment and then went storming off to another part of the ship. 'Whew!' Jane whispered. 'That was close!'

Jane escaped this time, but will she be so lucky the next time? Read Chapter Eight—and find out!

Chapter Eight

MORE WEEKS WENT by. Life upon the ship was hard for the two prisoners. Even Jane had almost given up hope of escaping from the pirates. Then, late one afternoon, they heard the man in the crow's nest shout, 'Land ho!'

Everyone rushed to the rail. There, far in the distance, land was in sight. As they sailed on, they could make out the outlines of a small city snuggled in a harbour. Coming closer they saw rocky cliffs lining the sides of the harbour and

steep mountains behind the town. 'We must escape,' cried Jane. 'This is our chance!'

'No way,' Tim murmured sadly. 'They'll lock us in the brig just as they did me when they attacked your town, Jane.'

'Then we must find a way to stay out of the brig,' Jane replied.

Just then Captain Redbeard approached. 'It'll be down in the brig with the two of you,' he said, laughing cruelly.

'Oh, Captain Redbeard,' Jane quickly answered. 'Don't put us in the brig when you attack the town. If there's a fight we may be able to help.'

'And how could you help?' snarled the Captain.

'We could bring food to the men,' said Jane.

'And we could make bandages in case
anyone got hurt,' added Tim, thinking
quickly.

Redbeard thought a minute. 'Aye,
that you could. All right now, I won't put
you in the brig, but keep out of the way
or I'll throw you both overboard!'

On deck the pirates raced to and fro,
preparing themselves for the attack on
the town. They loaded cannons,
sharpened swords and cleaned their
muskets. 'We must warn the

townspeople,' whispered Jane. 'They must know that the pirates are coming to attack.'

'But we can't run the Jolly Roger up this time. The Captain has it hidden away now.'

'Then we must do something else!' Jane said with determination.

By now they were closer to the town and could start to make out buildings and boats in the harbour. Their ship was sailing at full speed, straight towards the main wharf of the town. 'What can we do?' asked Tim. 'What can we do?'

'I know,' said Jane. 'Quick, we've got no time to lose!'

What will they do? Can they save the town? Or will the pirates succeed with their attack? Read Chapter Nine—and find out!

Chapter Nine

JANE AND TIM ran quickly through the swarm of busy pirates on deck. When no one was looking they climbed the ladder to the wheelhouse where the ship was steered with a great wooden wheel. Only one man was in the wheelhouse. Intent on keeping the ship on course, he stared straight ahead at the town. A bottle of rum stood on the deck just behind him and an empty one rolled around next to that.

Silently, Jane and Tim sneaked up behind him. Crouching just behind his legs they each picked up a bottle. Slowly they stood up, still unseen. Then, acting together, they quickly rose on tiptoe, raised the bottles high, and hit him on the head with them. Clunk! The man at the wheel fell to the floor unconscious.

Without saying a word to each other, Jane and Tim grabbed the heavy wheel and started to turn it as hard as they could. Slowly the ship began to veer from its course, away from the dock and towards the rocky cliffs that formed the side of the harbour. 'Hey, what's going on up there?' called Captain Redbeard to the wheelhouse. 'Somebody find out what's going on up there!'

But it was too late. Just as the pirate
reached the ladder, the ship crashed, full
speed, into the rocks. With a mighty roar
it smashed against the shore. Cannons,
hatch covers – everything went flying.
Many pirates fell overboard. Weighted
down by guns and swords, they

disappeared beneath the waves. The ship
started to break up in the pounding surf.
'Let's swim for it!' cried Tim.

'We'll never make it to the shore,' Jane
called above the sound of the waves as
they clung to each other in the slowly
tilting wheelhouse.

'You're right,' Tim answered. 'The
waves are too big. We can't swim in that
surf. We've saved the town, but it may
be the end of us.'

*Is this the end for Tim and Jane? Will
they perish in the foaming brine? Read
Chapter Ten—and find out!*

Chapter Ten

THE PIRATE SHIP was sinking fast.
Redbeard and some other pirates jumped
overboard and struggled to swim
through the heavy seas to shore. Tim
and Jane looked everywhere, trying to
find something to help them escape.

'I know!' said Jane suddenly. 'I see
something we can use for a raft.'

They raced down the ladder and onto
the deck. By this time the ship was half
under water and listing heavily to the
side. All the cannons had broken loose
from their moorings and were smashing
through the railings into the sea. A hatch
cover had broken loose and was lying
against the rail. 'Quick, Tim,' said Jane.
'Throw this over!'

Together they strained to move the

wooden cover. Lifting with all their might, they tilted the hatch cover over the rail and heaved it over the side. It splashed into the sea. Just as quickly the two whipped off their clothes and jumped in after it. They both landed alongside it and quickly pulled themselves on board. Grabbing a broken plank that floated nearby, Tim paddled for shore.

Their raft brought them safely through the waves. In a few minutes they felt it bump and scrape against a rock. Off they hopped and clambered up boulders to safety. By now the shore was lined with townspeople, come to see what the great commotion was about.

The people wrapped blankets around Tim and Jane and listened as they told the story of their capture and of their escape. 'Why, you saved the town,' said one. 'You are real heroes!'

They brought the two heroes back into town, warmed them in front of the fireplace at the inn and found clothes to fit them. Messengers were sent out to tell their parents that Jane and Tim were safe. They knew how happy their parents would be when they heard the good news.

But what of Redbeard and the pirates who tried to swim to shore? They struggled against the waves and were just about worn out when finally they reached land. Battered by the stormy seas, they hauled themselves onto the rocks and were instantly arrested, handcuffed, and marched off to prison.

As Redbeard passed Jane and Tim, still shivering in their blankets, he growled, 'You got me this time, mateys, but by my beard, I'm not done yet!'

That night the whole town threw a
party with Jane and Tim as the honoured
guests. There was a banquet for all in the
Town Hall. After the banquet everybody
spilled into the street. A band played
loudly, and everyone held hands and
danced in a great circle. Then the Mayor
told the band to stop. The people

gathered round as he made a long speech
about the bravery of the young girl and
boy.

At the end of his speech, he took two
velvet-covered boxes from his pocket.
One he gave to Jane and the other to
Tim. Excitedly they opened the boxes.
Inside each was a real gold medal which
said, 'To the bravest girl and boy in the

whole world'. Jane looked at Tim. They were both so happy. Tonight they were heroes. Soon they would be home with their families. And she knew that they would all live

Happily

Ever

After.